Dian
FOSSEY

Liz Gogerly

RAINTREE STECK-VAUGHN PUBLISHERS

A Harcourt Company

Austin   New York
www.raintreesteckvaughn.com

Copyright Permissions, Steck-Vaughn Company, P.O. Box 26015, Austin, TX 78755.

Published by Raintree Steck-Vaughn Publishers, an imprint of Steck-Vaughn Company

Library of Congress Cataloging-in-Publication Data

Gogerly, Liz.
 Dian Fossey/Liz Gogerly.
  p. cm.—(Scientists who made history)
 Includes bibliographical references (p.).
 Summary: Profiles the life of the scientist who studied mountain gorillas in central Africa and worked to ensure their survival.
 ISBN 0-7398-5225-6
  1. Fossey, Dian—Juvenile literature. 2. Primatologists—United States—Biography—Juvenile literature. 3. Gorilla—Rwanda—Juvenile literature. [1. Fossey, Dian. 2. Zoologists. 3. Gorilla. 4. Women—Biography.] I. Title. II. Series.

QL31.F65 G64 2002
599.884'092—dc21
[B]   2001058913

Printed in Italy. Bound in the United States.

1 2 3 4 5 6 7 8 9 0 LB 06 05 04 03 02

Picture Acknowledgments: Corbis 8, 17, 28; Dian Fossey Gorilla Fund 4, 5, 13, 16t, 20, 22, 23, 25, 27, 30, 32, 33, 35, 39; Impact Photos 21, 38, 40; Oxford Scientific Films 16b; Popperfoto 6, 7, 12, 29; Still Pictures 11, 14, 18, 19, 24, 26, 31, 37, 41; Topham Picturepoint 10, 34, 36.

Contents

"The Place of Hands"

THE SUN WAS shining brightly as Dian Fossey and *National Geographic Magazine* photographer Bob Campbell set off through the forest. They hadn't been following tracks for very long before they stumbled upon a group of gorillas that Fossey had named Group 8. The animals were feeding, and Fossey and Campbell watched as they chomped through the wild celery that they loved. Fossey experienced a warm glow. She felt privileged that these magnificent beasts were letting her into their lives. Peanuts, a bold young male, gave a quick display of branch slapping and chest beating, then lay down next to her to play.

LEFT: *A mountain gorilla in Rwanda, where Fossey carried out most of her research. Although she spent every day with the gorillas, it was three years before she made physical contact with one of these beautiful animals.*

LEFT: *Fossey was overjoyed when Peanuts first touched her hand. This picture shows the similarities between a gorilla's hand and our own.*

Bob quietly photographed the pair as they began to imitate each other. Soon Fossey lay down on the ground next to Peanuts. Gently she extended her hand toward the waiting gorilla, letting it drop to the floor. For a moment Peanuts looked unsure. Then, driven by his overwhelming curiosity, he reached out and his hand briefly covered Fossey's palm. It had finally happened! Fossey had tears in her eyes, and Peanuts was so excited that he made a proud little chest beat before bounding away into the forest. It was the first time a gorilla had dared to make contact with Fossey, and it had felt magical.

Fossey had encountered Peanuts and his group within a few months of arriving at Karisoke in Rwanda, Africa, in September 1967. Months later, he'd been the first gorilla to hold Fossey's gaze. Fossey had felt a flash of recognition and acceptance—he was as intrigued by her as she was by him. Since then, she had patiently watched Peanuts grow in confidence. Her patience was rewarded when he finally touched her hand on that sunny day in January 1970.

IN THEIR OWN WORDS

"Often I am asked about the most rewarding experience I have ever had with gorillas. The question is extremely difficult to answer because each hour with the gorillas provides its own return and satisfaction.... The [hand] contact was among the most memorable [experiences] of my life among the gorillas."

DIAN FOSSEY DESCRIBING HER FIRST CONTACT WITH A GORILLA IN HER BOOK *GORILLAS IN THE MIST*, 1983.

WILD THEORIES

In 1859, Charles Darwin's book *The Origin of Species* shocked the world. In it he suggested that humans may have evolved from apes. This outraged many people who believed that God had created humans. The debate about evolution continues to rage today.

Louis Leakey

In 1959, a paleoanthropologist named Louis Leakey discovered a skull of the earliest known ancestor of man in Tanzania, Africa. Believed to be 1.75 million years old, it showed that human evolution was much older than previously thought. Leakey went on to discover the remains of the two-million-year-old *Homo habilis*, which he considered the true ancestor of humans (*Homo sapiens*). These skeletons enabled him to piece together how our ancient ancestors moved and looked, but Leakey also wanted to find out about the evolution of human behavior.

Leakey thought that the close study of the chimpanzee, the gorilla, and the orangutan in their natural habitat would provide the key to human evolution. Studying apes to gain an insight into human behavior wasn't a new idea, but most studies had taken place in the laboratory. Those who'd tried to study chimpanzees in the wild had failed because the animals fled as soon as people came near. However, studies of the mountain gorillas in the Belgian Congo in Africa by George Schaller in 1959–1960 were promising, and in his book *The Year of the Gorilla* (1962), Schaller wrote about his encounters with these "amiable" (friendly) animals. Despite this success, many scientists thought Leakey was crazy to consider close-up studies.

ABOVE: *Although he traveled extensively, the scientist Charles Darwin (1809–1882) had little evidence for his theories of evolution. However, most scientists now believe his ideas to be correct.*

LEFT: *Dr. Louis Leakey (1903–1972) makes comparisons between the skull of a chimpanzee (left) and a skull of what is believed to be man's oldest ancestor. The humanlike skull was nicknamed "Nutcracker Man" because of its large teeth.*

His reputation didn't improve when he sent Jane Goodall, an unqualified young Englishwoman, to study the chimpanzees in the wild forests of Tanzania in July 1960. Only a few years later, Fossey was to follow in her footsteps.

JANE GOODALL AND THE GORILLAS

Rather than being wild and unpredictable, chimpanzees were found by Jane Goodall to be gentle with each other. They greet each other with hugs and kisses and tenderly groom each other. They also build soft, leafy nests to sleep in. She discovered that, like humans, chimpanzees sometimes hunt for meat and use natural vegetation as tools or weapons. For example, when they're eating thorny plants, they use leaves to hold the stem and protect their hands. Jane recorded all her observations in journals. Rather than follow the accepted scientific approach, with numbers and statistics, Jane talked about the animals as individuals. Many scientists criticized this method, but none could deny its success.

IN THEIR OWN WORDS

"Dr. Leakey spoke to me most enthusiastically about Jane Goodall's excellent fieldwork with the chimpanzees....I believe it was at this time the seed was planted in my head ... that I would someday return to Africa to study the gorillas."

DIAN FOSSEY WRITING ABOUT HER FIRST MEETING WITH DR. LOUIS LEAKEY IN *GORILLAS IN THE MIST.*

Lonely Years

DIAN FOSSEY WAS born on January 16, 1932, in Fairfax, California, near San Francisco. She was the only child of George and Kitty Fossey. When Dian was six her parents divorced, and a year later her mother married a man named Richard Price. Dian's father tried to stay in contact with her, but since he wasn't well liked in the Price household, they soon lost touch altogether. Dian's upbringing was very strict, and despite her pleas for a pet dog or cat, she was only allowed a goldfish.

Dian's lonely childhood was followed by years of working her own way through college. In 1950, she began a course in pre-veterinary medicine at the University of California in

BELOW: *Fossey loved to spend time in the forests of Kentucky. It was here that she first became passionate about wildlife.*

Davis. Without her parents' financial backing, she had to take temporary jobs in factories, offices, or laboratories. Although she was determined to work with animals, she found science very difficult. When she failed her second year, she was forced to rethink her plans. By 1954, Dian had received a degree in occupational therapy, and she spent the next seven years as director of occupational therapy at a hospital for disabled children in Louisville, Kentucky.

In Kentucky, Dian found some happiness. She moved to a cottage on a farm called Glenmary on the outskirts of Louisville. Surrounded by forests and fields, Dian found she enjoyed the peace and quiet. She also discovered that watching the farm animals and wild creatures in the countryside interested her. She was slowly moving toward her true calling in life.

IN THEIR OWN WORDS

"When I wake up in the morning, I just run to the windows all over the house and am blinded by the beauty."

DIAN FOSSEY TALKING ABOUT HER TIME AT GLENMARY FARM IN *GORILLAS IN THE MIST*, 1983.

The Call of Africa

FOR YEARS, FOSSEY had dreamed of visiting Africa. Friends returned from the African bush with exciting tales about the wild animals, and she wanted to see them for herself. As usual, money was an obstacle, but she was determined to experience Africa for herself by the end of 1963. Eventually she decided to take out a three-year loan to fund a six-week safari to Kenya, Tanzania, Uganda, and Southern Rhodesia (now Zimbabwe).

Reading about Africa and preparations for the trip occupied Fossey for the months leading up to her dream trip. One book, George Schaller's *The Year of the Gorilla*, particularly interested her. Fossey wanted to see the majestic mountain gorillas he talked about for herself, so she added the Congo (now Democratic Republic of Congo) to her itinerary. As Fossey's excitement grew, so did her fears for her health. She had always suffered from bouts of pneumonia, and was especially worried that the pneumonia that struck a month before she was due to leave would affect her plans. Despite her weakened state, Fossey boarded the plane to Kenya on September 26, 1963.

BELOW: *This photograph of a gorilla was taken by George Schaller, whose work fascinated Fossey.*

ABOVE: *Africa cast its spell on Fossey. Although she fell in love with the gorillas, she was also enchanted by many other species, including elephants and impalas.*

Unsurprisingly, Fossey fell in love with Africa. Seeing animals in their natural habitats filled her with wonder. Of all the African creatures, though, the mountain gorillas she saw in the Virungas Volcanoes region in the Congo moved her the most. When she heard their high-pitched screams, then finally saw them, she was overwhelmed. She knew that she'd have to return to Africa one day. A meeting with the paleoanthropologist Louis Leakey in Tanzania added to her determination to return. Leakey had admired the gutsy American woman who claimed she wanted to come back to Africa to work with the gorillas, and he told her to keep in touch.

IN THEIR OWN WORDS

"I was struck by the physical magnificence of the huge jet-black bodies blended against the green ... of the thick forest foliage."

FOSSEY REMEMBERING THE FIRST TIME SHE SAW A MOUNTAIN GORILLA IN THE WILD.

"GORILLA GIRL"

Fossey's enthusiasm for her African adventure was shown in magazine articles that were published in Louisville's *Courier Journal*, together with photographs she had taken of the mountain gorillas. However, it wasn't until three years later, in March 1966, that she had the opportunity to discuss her passion with Louis Leakey again. Leakey was visiting Louisville, and Fossey was amazed when he recognized her and requested a meeting.

Leakey had been looking for a suitable person to conduct long-term close-up research of mountain gorillas in the Virungas Volcanos. He particularly liked using women for his studies and felt that Jane Goodall had more than proven that women had the necessary patience and determination to do the job well. In Fossey he saw a strong-willed woman who was mature and dedicated enough to handle the rigors of living in the wilds of Africa for a long period of time. However, Fossey was shocked when Leakey concluded their meeting by suggesting that she have her appendix removed. He pointed out that appendicitis could be deadly if it struck when medical help wasn't readily available.

LEFT: *Jane Goodall makes friends with a chimpanzee in Tanzania. During her studies, she made constant comparisons between human and chimp behavior. Examples of DNA suggest the chimpanzee might be humans' closest living relative.*

Fossey, who had not been offered the job officially, promptly had her appendix removed, and waited for Leakey to contact her. When his letter arrived, it was a dream come true. Leakey wanted Fossey as his "gorilla girl"—he would find sponsors for the costs of travel and setting up a research base. In return, she would write about her experiences with the gorillas. Later he told Fossey that he'd suggested she have her appendix removed only as a joke. But the determination she displayed in having the operation made him sure that he'd found the right woman for the job.

ABOVE: *Although Fossey knew that life in the the remote jungles of central Africa would be difficult, she couldn't wait to begin her work there.*

IN THEIR OWN WORDS

"There was no way that I could explain to dogs, friends, or parents my compelling need to return to Africa to launch a long-term study of gorillas. Some may call it destiny and others may call it dismaying. I call the sudden turn of events in my life fortuitous [lucky]."

DIAN FOSSEY TALKING ABOUT LEAVING THE UNITED STATES
IN *GORILLAS IN THE MIST.*

INTO THE WILDERNESS

In December 1966, Fossey was on a plane bound for Africa once again. Since Leakey's letter had arrived, she'd faced more obstacles. Pneumonia struck yet again, and her parents put up strong objections to her living alone in the politically unstable Congo. But Fossey was determined. As she set off for the airport, she was weighed down with four cameras, a typewriter with paper, and a whole wardrobe of outdoor clothes.

Leakey had arranged for Fossey to spend Christmas with Jane Goodall and her husband. Jane had been studying the chimpanzees at Gombe in Tanzania for over three years, and she gave Fossey a crash course in data collection. Then, before journeying to the Virungas, Fossey met Leakey in Kenya. There they bought a secondhand Land Rover, which Fossey later named Lily.

MOUNTAIN GORILLAS

People have known about the existence of the gorilla since the 19th century, but it wasn't until 1902 that the mountain gorilla (*Gorilla gorilla beringei*) was discovered. There are two other subspecies of gorilla, called the western lowland gorilla (*Gorilla gorilla gorilla*) and the eastern lowland gorilla (*Gorilla gorilla grauen*). Mountain gorillas live only in the mountain rain forests in central Africa. They are similar to the other subspecies, but are larger and more muscular. The adult male can be 5'7"–5'11" (1.7–1.8 m) tall when standing. They live in groups that vary in size from about 3 to 38 members. A group has one adult male over 15 years old. This majestic creature is called a silverback, because of his silvery fur. He takes charge of a group that includes young adult males, several females, and their offspring.

ABOVE: *A silverback mountain gorilla is usually twice as heavy as an adult female and armed with longer teeth.*

ABOVE: *This map shows the countries Fossey visited in Africa, and their neighboring countries.*
TOP: *A map of the Virungas National Park, showing the places where Fossey lived and worked.*

Journey to the Congo

By chance, Fossey also met the photographer Alan Root while in Kenya. He accompanied her on the 700-mile trip to the Congo. They passed through dense jungle, savannah, and stretches of wilderness before arriving in the heart of Africa—the Congo. Fossey was determined to go back to Kabara in the Virungas; it was where she had first seen gorillas and where George Schaller had studied the animals in 1960. It was also an area of political unrest; rebellion against the government of Congo meant that foreign travelers were in danger.

However, nothing would dampen Fossey's determination. Accompanied by Root, she hired men to take them up the 4,000 feet to the Kabara meadow. At their journey's end, Fossey breathed in the sweet mountain air, looked across at the string of volcanoes, and hugged herself with joy. She knew that she'd soon be with the gorillas again.

IN THEIR OWN WORDS

"There were vistas [views] along the trail that left me speechless with their majesty. The far sweep of volcanoes seemed never to end. There were some wondrous, sprawling hagenia trees lining the trail that seemed so familiar I wanted to rush up to them to shake branches."

FOSSEY TALKS ABOUT HER RETURN TO KABARA IN *WOMAN IN THE MISTS* BY FARLEY MOWAT, 1988.

WAKING UP TO NATURE

Alan Root gave Fossey invaluable lessons in tracking, but after two days he had to leave the camp. Fossey was anxious about being alone, but her fears were eased a few days later with the arrival of Sanwekwe, a Congolese tracker. She'd met Sanwekwe on her previous trip; he'd worked for George Schaller and Fossey had admired his skills as a tracker.

ABOVE: *Fossey's camp at Kabara was far away from civilization. She had a small shortwave radio, but listening to the outside world often made her feel even lonelier.*

TRACKING GORILLAS

Successful tracking of gorillas takes great patience and experience. Gorillas are terrestrial, which means they travel mainly on the ground. They "knuckle walk"—so they appear to walk on all fours—and they leave knuckleprints in the ground as they travel. These prints, together with trails of fresh dung and the disruption of trees and plants, provide clues to their whereabouts. Fossey discovered other ways of finding her gorillas, though. By crawling through the undergrowth close to the ground she could detect smells. The great silverbacks had a distinctive body odor, much like strong human sweat, which clung to the vegetation.

ABOVE: *A gorilla knuckleprint.*

On the morning of January 19, 1967, Fossey and Sanwekwe left camp early and had their first lengthy gorilla sighting. For three hours they were transfixed as a group of nine gorillas went about their daily business. In between sunning themselves in the hot patches of the forest, they barked, hooted, and squealed, as well as making their distinctive chest beat, which echoed through the forest with a "pok-pok" sound. From now on, each movement and sound the animals made would be recorded and typed up by Fossey every evening. Like Jane Goodall, she didn't want to record the animals' activities as a series of checkmarks on a chart; she wanted to write about their everyday lives almost as if they were stories.

Life on the mountain wasn't easy. Years of frequent pneumonia had weakened Fossey's lungs, and the long treks through the forests at high altitude were difficult. With her clothes constantly dampened from the misty mountain air, she also became ill more easily. She made monthly trips to the nearest village at the foot of the mountains for fresh vegetables and fruit, but these soon ran out. It was only Fossey's determination and love for the gorillas that kept her focused on her job.

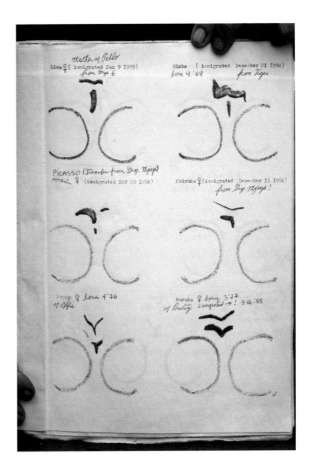

ABOVE: *A page of Fossey's handwritten notes and diagrams of gorilla noseprints. She took pleasure in recording the small details of the gorillas' behavior and lives.*

IN THEIR OWN WORDS

"Because of the near daily encounters with elephant, buffalo, giant forest hog, and, of course, gorilla, the time spent in the field was by far more exciting than the hours, that, of necessity, had to be spent in camp. Almost immediately, I became bogged down in paperwork and have remained that way ever since."

FOSSEY IN *GORILLAS IN THE MIST*.

FRIENDS AND FOES

"The Kabara groups taught me much regarding gorilla behavior. From them I learned to accept the animals on their own terms and never to push them beyond the varying levels of tolerance they were willing to give."

DIAN FOSSEY IN *GORILLAS IN THE MIST*.

It took time to gain the trust of the mountain gorillas, and Fossey made mistakes. If she came too close too soon, or without warning, the silverbacks would charge at her or take their group and flee. Fossey eventually found that it was better that the gorillas saw her first and then, in their own time, they would inch closer to her. She also discovered that imitating the sounds they made was more successful than talking to them. She gradually learned which sounds gained the animals' confidence.

When Fossey began her observations, she had slapped her thighs in imitation of their chestbeats. She soon realized that this was a sign of excitement or fear for gorillas, and that it was better to copy their contentment vocalizations, which sounded like a purr. Fossey also copied the animals' movements. Scratching, pretending to eat the wild celery they liked, or even crouching in a submissive position all helped to win their trust.

RIGHT: *A female gorilla beats her chest. This is usually a sign of excitement.*

GORILLA TALK

Gorillas communicate using body language and sounds. Fossey discovered 25 distinct sounds or vocalizations. She quickly learned the difference between the sounds. Roars tend to be aggressive, while screams and "wraaghs" are to raise alarm in any situation. High-pitched barking usually expresses mild alarm and curiosity—Fossey often heard this response when she was found hiding in the bushes. One of the most comforting sounds Fossey discovered is the belch vocalization, which often means that the gorillas are contented. She particularly enjoyed hearing the gorillas chuckle, which they do when they're playing. Sounds to communicate with other groups include the hootseries, or "hoo-hoo-hoos," which often come before chestbeats.

As Fossey made progress with the gorillas, events in the human world began to take over. On July 9, 1967, armed Congolese soldiers arrived at the camp. A rebel leader, Moise Tshombe, had taken the leadership of the eastern region of the Congo by force. The border between the Congo and Uganda had been closed, and white people were being treated with great mistrust. After six months of study, Fossey was escorted down the mountain and taken into custody.

It was now too dangerous to stay in the Congo. Many people, including Leakey, pleaded with Fossey to return to the United States, but Fossey was determined to transfer her studies to a grassy clearing a short distance from Kabara in Rwanda. Rwanda is located a few miles south of the equator, and is one of the smallest countries in Africa. By September 24, 1967, Fossey had found her new research camp; it was 10,000 feet up in the Rwandan National Park, between the mountains of Karisimbi and Visoke—she called it Karisoke.

ABOVE: *A mother gorilla is photographed vocalizing to her baby. Fossey soon learned that different vocalizations had very different meanings.*

The Camp at Karisoke

THE CAMP AT Karisoke was in a clearing surrounded by forest, with a stream flowing through it. As the first tents were put up, Fossey heard gorilla chestbeats—and she knew she had found the right place for her research. However, Karisoke would be quite different from Kabara. Rwanda is a heavily populated country and its people (the Batwa, the Hutu, and the Tutsi tribes) farm and graze within the national park. From now on, Fossey would make many friends within the gorilla community, but she would also make many enemies of the farmers and poachers who threatened the gorilla's natural habitat.

The most important thing to Fossey was contact with the gorillas. At Karisoke, the gorillas were more wary of humans. After a year of study, the animals were still unused to Fossey, who would wait patiently, sitting 30 to 40 feet away.

ABOVE: *At first, Fossey lived in tents at Karisoke. Later she moved into this cabin. She made curtains out of African material and put tusks, animal skins, and pictures on the walls.*

IDENTIFYING GORILLAS

As Fossey began to recognize the gorillas in each group, she gave them names. She quickly found ways of distinguishing between them because every gorilla has its own noseprint (see page 17). While the noses of animals in the same group are similar, each gorilla has a slightly different nose. Fossey would make sketches of each noseprint. Other vital clues to identification included coloring. Mountain gorillas have long fur that varies in color from blue-black to brownish-gray. Fossey also watched for distinguishing features such as scars or birthmarks—much the same as humans do on passports. She called her favorite gorilla Digit, because he had lost a finger.

Gorilla Groups

During her eighteen years of research at Karisoke, Fossey encountered nine groups of gorillas. Each group was numbered, and every individual was given a name. Fossey concentrated her studies on three groups: Groups 4, 5, and 8. The dominant silverback, usually about twice the size of the adult females, was the leader of each group. He would lead a group through the forests, his experience determining his reaction to each situation. If the situation was threatening, he might lead his group to charge the enemy. However, Fossey found that once a silverback had grown used to her presence, the younger members of his group would come to her. It was almost as if the great silverback had allowed the youngsters out to play with a friend. Eventually it was the silverback's trust that allowed her to observe the gorillas.

IN THEIR OWN WORDS

"Once within sight of Rafiki, the elderly female moved directly to him. They looked directly into each other's face and embraced. She placed her arm over his back and he did likewise over hers."

DIAN FOSSEY REMEMBERING AN AFFECTIONATE MOMENT BETWEEN THE SILVERBACK RAFIKI AND THE OLD MATRIARCH COCO IN GROUP 8.

LEFT: *After waking at about 6 A.M., most family groups spend the morning feeding. By noon they are ready for a rest, although the youngsters often like to play.*

FAMILY TIES

All gorillas were important to Fossey, but she grew especially close to certain individuals, such as Peanuts (see pages 4–5). Of all the gorillas, Fossey's favorite was Digit of Group 4. She watched him grow and develop from a five-year-old, bouncy bundle of black fluff to a young adult who was beginning to take responsibility for protecting the group.

When Fossey first encountered Group 4 in 1967, there had been fourteen members. The silverback leader was an elderly giant she called Whinny. The group contained two senior females, as well as four young adult females, aged between six and eight. Two younger silverbacks, a few infants, and young adult males, including Digit, completed the group.

ABOVE: *Members of Group 4 play in the undergrowth. Although young gorillas enjoy a game, they never venture far away from their mother.*

By 1972, Fossey was spending a great deal of time with Group 4 and had gathered much information about its behavior. Whinny had died of natural causes in 1968, and now the fifteen-year-old silverback, Uncle Bert, was the relatively young and inexperienced leader. Uncle Bert's youthfulness meant he enjoyed playing. Playtime, Fossey discovered, was extremely important to the younger gorillas. They enjoyed leaping from tree to tree and having long wrestling matches. She loved watching their antics, and they often included her in their games, allowing her to tickle or groom them.

Unfortunately, Uncle Bert's inexperience often led Group 4 into fights with other groups. Intergroup interaction, when two different groups of gorillas come together, is a necessary part of gorilla survival. However, sexually mature females are often poached from one group to ensure the survival of another. The meetings can be violent, and many animals are injured or killed defending their groups. Eventually Uncle Bert lost three young females to another group.

IN THEIR OWN WORDS

"He comes right up to my side, plops down, and, looking me directly in the eyes, begins very seriously a long tirade of relating past events, injustices by his family, how the weather has been treating them, and on it goes. All done in soft drones and hums, sometimes with mouth opening and closing as though he were trying to imitate human conversation."

DIAN FOSSEY WRITES ABOUT PUCK FROM GROUP 5
IN A LETTER TO HER FRIENDS, THE SCHWARTZELS,
FROM *WALKING WITH THE GREAT APES*
BY SY MONTGOMERY, 1991.

RIGHT: *Fossey tried to type up her notes about the day's events every night. A rescued monkey named Kima often kept her company.*

BRINGING UP BABIES

Infant gorillas are breastfed by their mothers until they are about two years old. Fossey especially enjoyed observing the gorillas raise their offspring. In February 1969, she heard that a baby gorilla had been trapped by poachers to send to a German zoo. She was furious, and persuaded the park guard (called a conservator) to let her take the baby back to Karisoke.

Coco and Pucker

The capture of infant gorillas is a particularly horrible business. In order to snatch a baby, many members of the gorilla group are killed as they try to protect their young.

Fossey was determined to help the rescued infant recover from its ordeal. She named it Coco and put her in a room next to her own at Karisoke. The room was decorated with forest vegetation that gorillas particularly like to eat, and soft vegetation on which Coco could nest. Once they were alone, Fossey opened Coco's pen. To her amazement, Coco crawled onto her lap. Later, when Coco looked out the window at the mountains, she started sobbing. It would be the only time that Fossey saw a gorilla cry.

LEFT: *A baby gorilla is eating leaves. Fossey fed Coco and Pucker a natural diet of wild celery, thistles, and nettles.*

Fossey dedicated herself to Coco's survival. She reassured the frightened animal with gorilla vocalizations, and sometimes cuddled her to sleep. Like a human child, Coco responded to the warmth and feeling of security. A week later she was making a steady recovery, when another baby gorilla was brought to the camp. Pucker had been captured as a replacement for the German zoo. All eight of her family group had died trying to save her.

Months of loving attention saved both gorillas, but Fossey knew she couldn't prevent them from being sent to Germany. When the time came for their departure, Fossey packed the last forest vegetation she knew they would ever eat into their cage. Through the years, Fossey saw photographs and heard stories about her "wild orphans." They looked and sounded depressed. Then in 1978, at only age ten, Coco and Pucker died within a month of each other.

BELOW: *Fossey is stroking a gorilla's foot. After her experience with Coco and Pucker, she often used touch to communicate with the gorillas.*

IN THEIR OWN WORDS

"After a few weeks I changed approaches from mild 'tickle-tickles' to drawn-out 'ouchy-gouchy-goo-zoooom'. . . . The term 'ouchy-gouchy-goo-zoooom' is not in any dictionary, yet it seems to be an international. . . term that can evoke laughter and smiles from both human and nonhuman primates."

DIAN FOSSEY WRITING ABOUT THE TICKLING GAMES SHE ENJOYED WITH COCO AND PUCKER IN *GORILLAS IN THE MIST*.

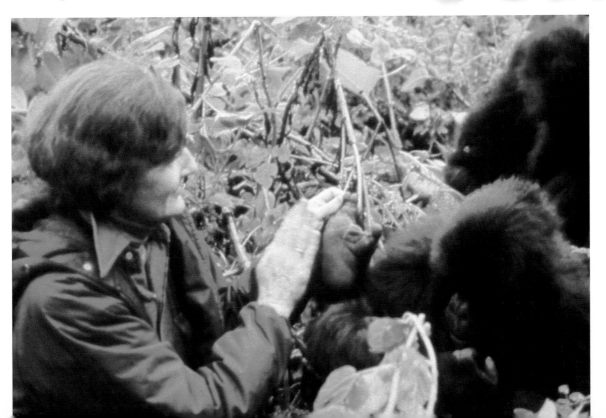

THE FIGHT FOR LIFE

When Fossey founded Karisoke, she knew that the local people herded cattle and hunted within the park. She told them that she would not tolerate either activity in the study areas. Friends tried to make her be sensible; the locals, after all, had always herded cattle in the park and they hunted for meat to feed their families. Fossey argued that they kept too many cattle and began herding away the cattle that strayed onto "her" area. She also destroyed any traps she found laid down by the poachers. They not only killed the wildlife, she reasoned, they also trapped the gorillas.

Fossey grew angrier when it became clear that gorillas were becoming game for the tourist trade. Not only did poachers catch infants to sell overseas to zoos, but they killed adult gorillas to sell as body parts—ashtrays made from gorillas' hands were particularly popular. In 1970, while Fossey was away in England, she heard about the massacre of five adult gorillas on the outskirts of the park. There was little Fossey could do but write angry letters to the park director and conservation organizations.

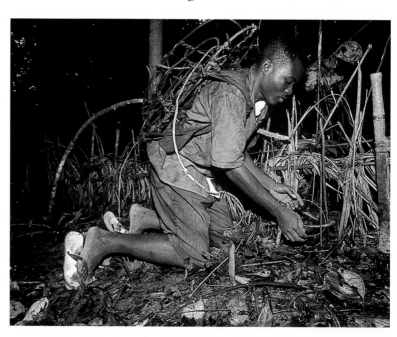

RIGHT: *A poacher is setting an animal trap. Gorillas were often caught in wire traps or deep pit traps with pointed stakes at the bottom.*

LEFT: *This gorilla has lost a hand in a snare. Some gorillas die later of an infection from their injuries.*

The local people were already suspicious of Fossey. They called her Nyiramachabelli—the old woman who lives alone in the forest without a man. Now she became even more unpopular as she took the herding and poaching problem into her own hands. In July 1973, after they had driven cattle into a local settlement, she pulled a gun on locals. On other occasions, she shot at and killed cattle. Sometimes she held poachers hostage and bullied them into revealing information about their employers. She'd then spook them using halloween masks and firecrackers, as she pretended to be a witch. The locals believed in black magic, or *sumu* as they called it, and began to fear and dislike this unpredictable woman.

Fame and Fury

IN ORDER TO receive further grants for her research, Fossey needed a Ph.D. (doctorate in philosophy). Between January 1970 and 1976, when her thesis was accepted, she made regular trips to Cambridge University in England to get a doctorate in zoology. Her dissertation was based upon her research with the gorillas. She had to be away from Africa for months at a time and missed the gorillas terribly. As the poachers moved in and her conservation work became more important, she was forced to recruit researchers to continue her work during her absence. However, not everybody had the same commitment to conservation as Fossey, and this added to her worries while she was away.

The National Geographic Society had always supported Fossey's work by paying for the upkeep of the camp. In return, her story and the progress of her research was regularly featured in *National Geographic* magazine.

LEFT: *Fossey spent her time at Cambridge University studying and worrying about the gorillas back at Karisoke.*

ABOVE:
*Photographs of
Fossey and the gorillas,
such as this one, taken for the
National Geographic Society,
helped develop public interest
in her work.*

In the January 1970 issue, beautiful color photographs of
the gorillas in their natural habitat had introduced Fossey
and her work to the world. She was filmed by the National
Geographic Society in 1968, 1969, and 1970, and in later years
television cameras from around the world filmed the gorillas.
In 1978, British television host David Attenborough was filmed
with the gorillas for the British Broadcasting Corporation
(BBC) *Life on Earth* series. Now everybody could see what
Fossey already knew—that these majestic creatures were as
gentle as they were strong, and that there was a recognition
between our two species that went both ways.

Fossey hated the disturbance to the lives of the gorillas
that such publicity brought, but she recognized there could
be a benefit. When poaching became a serious problem, she
threatened to use her fame to generate international
disapproval. It was a promise she kept. She also insisted she'd
find out who was behind the killings. Dian Fossey was not
only becoming famous, she was turning into a serious threat
to the Rwandan authorities. From now on, they started to
monitor her movements.

IN THEIR OWN WORDS

*"In their greed to obtain
photographs, tourists and
uninvited film crews came
to pose almost as much of a
threat to the gorillas as
poachers did. One French
film team...relentlessly
pursued Group 5 daily for
six weeks. The trauma
caused Effie to abort [lose
her unborn baby]."*

FOSSEY IN *GORILLAS IN THE MIST*, 1983.

DEATH OF A GENTLE FRIEND

IN THEIR OWN WORDS

"If I was alone, he often invited play by flopping over onto his back, waving stumpy legs in the air, and looking at me smilingly as if to say, 'How can you resist me?' At such times, I fear, my scientific detachment dissolved."

DIAN FOSSEY WRITING ABOUT DIGIT IN
GORILLAS IN THE MIST.

In January 1978, Fossey had been preparing to welcome David Attenborough and the BBC film crew. She wanted to make a good impression, but by the time the BBC had arrived there had been a terrible discovery. On December 31, 1977, the poachers targeted one of Fossey's gorilla groups—Group 4—for the first time. Digit was now ten years old, and was taking some responsibility for defending the group. It seemed that he had been attacked as he fought off the poachers. When his body was discovered in early January 1978, it had been hacked almost beyond recognition. Fossey was wracked with grief. She replayed the scenes of their friendship in her mind. She remembered him as the gentle and curious animal who'd lain his head in her lap. She was now more determined than ever to put a stop to the poachers.

RIGHT: *Fossey's favorite gorilla, Digit, had been filmed by* National Geographic *as he rolled over and slept. It is possible that his trust in human beings made him an easy target for the poachers.*

Fossey wrote to the Rwandan president, Major General Juvenal Habyarimana, telling him that she would contact every conservation society she could reach in her quest to protect the gorillas. She would ask them to pressure the Rwandan government to cut funds to the park conservator and guards, since they didn't do their job. She also suggested that stronger penalties for the poachers, such as long prison sentences or even death, might deter their actions.

Later Fossey mounted a poster campaign that showed Digit's mutilated body, saying "Come and Visit Me in Rwanda." It was a copy of a poster that had used a photograph of Digit to promote tourism in Rwanda. Finally she launched an international fund-raising campaign that would become known as the Digit Fund. The money collected would be used for anti-poaching patrols. From this point on, Fossey's work would center on active conservation. This would prove to be a dangerous business that made her many enemies.

ABOVE: *Fossey's anti-poaching campaign helped raise awareness of the dangers of poaching throughout Africa. This anti-poaching patrol is working in Tanzania, which shares a border with Rwanda.*

MAKING ENEMIES

Sadly the anti-poaching patrols could not be put in place quickly enough to save other members in Group 4. Uncle Bert, the silverback leader, and a young mother named Macho were shot in July 1978. The poachers wanted to snatch Macho's son, Kweli, but, miraculously, Fossey later found the infant. However, without its silverback leader, Group 4 was in danger of being poached by other groups. In time, the group would cease to exist.

IN THEIR OWN WORDS

"She was very wary about entering into a relationship. The gorillas...were honest in their feelings toward her. If they were angry, you could see they were angry; if they liked you, they showed it. It was very up front. Fossey appreciated the honesty of the relationship you have with gorillas, and you don't owe them anything and they don't owe you anything, other than trust. With the gorillas she didn't have to hide her feelings from them."

IAN REDMOND, FOSSEY'S FRIEND AND COLLEAGUE, FROM *WALKING WITH THE GREAT APES* BY SY MONTGOMERY.

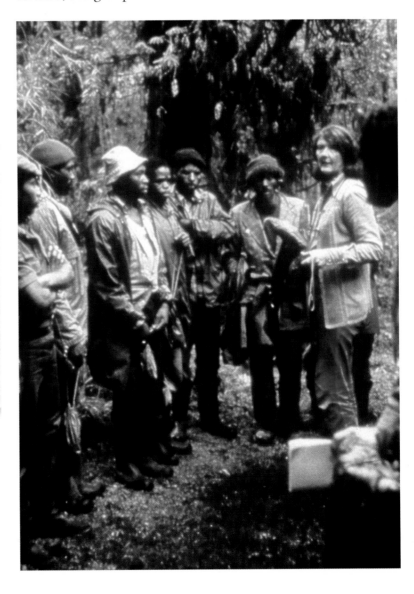

RIGHT: *Fossey organizes an anti-poaching patrol at Karisoke. She declared all-out war against the poachers, who she believed were responsible for the death of two-thirds of the gorillas in her study area.*

Fossey began to suffer from her fragile health again. Over the years, climbing at such high altitudes took away her breath, and she'd been struck by many illnesses including rabies, dysentery, and pneumonia. Furthermore, the loss of so many gorillas to poachers made her angry and depressed.

Some people felt Fossey's behavior was becoming more and more unpredictable and irresponsible. She was suspicious of everybody, including the park conservator. She thought he might be employing poachers, then using the slaughter of animals as a reason to ask for more funding for the park. She also discriminated against African project workers who were helping with her research. If the gorillas became used to black researchers, she believed they would be less likely to run from poachers, who were also black. This reasoning seemed racist and angered the people in whose land she was actually a visitor.

ABOVE: *Gorillas often have mannerisms or facial expressions that are similar to those of humans, which makes them especially appealing to tourists. Fossey believed that tourism posed a major threat to the gorillas' survival.*

Fossey was also increasingly against the gorilla safaris that had become an important part of Rwandan tourism. She was particularly upset that Group 5 had moved from the safety of the poacher-free zone to the outskirts of the park to avoid the tourists. By 1979, many people thought it would be better for the future of Karisoke if Fossey left. With Fossey in charge, funding was becoming a problem. Because of the bad publicity, even the National Geographic Society wanted Fossey to leave Rwanda.

Gorillas in the Mist

WITHOUT HELP FROM the National Geographic Society, Fossey realized she would have to leave Karisoke. An offer to teach at Cornell University in Ithaca, New York, in 1980 gave her a reason to leave. While in the United States she could also write her book, which she later called *Gorillas in the Mist*. Fossey's portrait of her life and the lives of the gorillas she watched for thirteen years is an absorbing adventure story. It introduces the different family groups and the "wild orphans" Coco and Pucker. When *Gorillas in the Mist* was published in 1983, the book was an international success. Fossey was delighted that she had been able to bring the gorillas to life for so many readers.

ABOVE: *A group of students having a class discussion on the campus of Cornell University, where Fossey taught for several years in the early 1980s.*

LEFT: *Sandy Harcourt (left) with another researcher and Fossey (right). Harcourt ran Karisoke while Fossey was in the United States.*

During these years in the United States, Fossey managed to rebuild her strength. Despite her severely damaged lungs and bad back, the call of Africa was still strong. She worried about the state of Karisoke, which was being run in her absence by a scientist named Sandy Harcourt. Fossey distrusted his more scientific approach to research, and she particularly worried about the plight of the gorillas.

News that another silverback had been slaughtered trying to protect its young reached her in December 1982. Fossey was desperate to fly out immediately, but because of her work at Cornell, she wouldn't return to Karisoke until the following June. On her arrival in Karisoke, Fossey found that the gorillas needed her more than ever. The camp had been badly neglected by the visiting scientists, and Fossey despaired at the work ahead of her. Her spirits were lifted by a warm welcome from Group 5. When the whole group came to meet her she was ecstatic—she was really home!

IN THEIR OWN WORDS

"She stared intently into my eyes, and it was eye-to-eye contact for thirty or forty seconds. Not knowing quite what to do, for I had never had this reaction from gorillas before, I squished myself flat on the bed of vegetation. Whereupon she smelled my head and neck, then lay down beside me ... and embraced me! ... GOD, she did remember."

FOSSEY'S THRILLED RESPONSE TO MEETING HER OLD FRIEND TUCK.

THE FIGHT GOES ON

Toward the end of August 1983, Fossey was attending lecture tours in the United States to publicize *Gorillas in the Mist*. While there she came up with a new way to protect the gorillas. She called it the Guardians for Gorillas Groups. People from overseas would adopt a gorilla group, and the money raised would be used to pay local people to protect the gorillas. By paying them to protect the animals, the locals would have no need to poach them anymore.

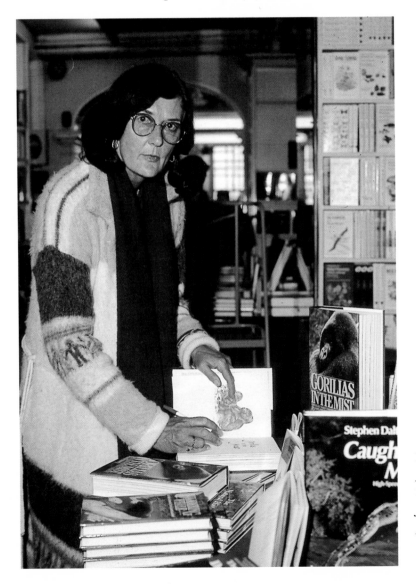

LEFT: *The strain of another promotional tour for* Gorillas in the Mist *shows on Fossey's face in this February 1984 photograph. By the end of the month, she was back at Karisoke again.*

Meanwhile, the research project at Karisoke went bankrupt and was in danger of being closed down. By December, Fossey was back in Karisoke and in control. Using the money she'd earned on the lecture tour and proceeds from her book, she managed to pay the camp staff and trackers who kept the camp going. Money from the Digit Fund meant that anti-poaching patrols still managed to ruin traps and protect the gorillas from poachers, too.

With Fossey's health becoming worse, it grew more difficult for her to visit the gorillas in the mountains. She was particularly worried about their changing behavior and the shifting social structure within the groups. It was usual for young males to split off to form new groups, but now female members of groups were leaving groups to search for males. This unusual behavior was creating friction within the groups. Fossey called these strange episodes "Gorilla Soap Opera," but she was deeply concerned about the long-term effects upon the gorilla community of humans taking over their habitat.

IN THEIR OWN WORDS

"I'm going to die and the gorillas will all die around me. They'll be gone within ten years."

FOSSEY'S PREDICTION FOR HERSELF AND THE GORILLAS, FROM *WALKING WITH THE GREAT APES* BY SY MONTGOMERY.

The Killers in the Mist

IN MAY 1985, the anti-poaching patrols caught Sebahutu, a well-known poacher. Fossey tied him up in her living room for a day until he gave her the names of sixty poachers, as well as others who were involved in the selling of animals. There were many important people on that list. Perhaps it was Sebahutu's information that would eventually endanger Fossey's life.

ABOVE: *The last pictures of Fossey were taken outside her hut in Karisoke with camp workers and anti-poaching patrollers. In front of them is a giant pile of snares and traps they have collected.*

However, Fossey was preoccupied with fund-raising for Karisoke, and in June she left for the United States to collect money raised by the Digit Fund. While she was away, the Rwandan president's son visited Karisoke. He was told that Fossey was keeping tourists away from the gorillas. Since the gorilla safaris were an important part of Rwanda's income, he became angry.

On Fossey's return to Karisoke, a series of weird events had an unsettling effect on her. She had always taken the locals' use of black magic seriously. Years earlier when she had discovered that her hair was being collected for use in spells against her, she began to clean her hairbrush every night. In October 1985, when her pet parrots were poisoned, she began to feel afraid. Later, when she found a wooden carving of a puff adder, a venomous species of snake, she knew that the locals were practicing their black magic upon her—a puff adder was a death curse!

Fossey's health was becoming even worse; she was now coughing up blood. Her health had been so bad for years that there was no reason to suspect witchcraft was the cause, but Fossey still wondered....However, even Fossey could not have guessed what would follow. After spending a quiet Christmas at Karisoke, Fossey was found brutally murdered in her hut on December 27, 1985.

IN THEIR OWN WORDS

"When you realize the value of all life, you dwell less on what is past and concentrate more on the preservation of the future."

FOSSEY'S FINAL LETTER TO HER FRIEND
ROSAMUND CARR, DECEMBER 22, 1985.

ABOVE: *Fossey's living room had been her sanctuary. The walls were covered in photographs of her friends, the gorillas. Her body was found in the next room, beside her bed.*

THE END IN SIGHT

Fossey was buried next to Digit on December 31, 1985, in the little gorilla graveyard that she had started. Her simple gravestone was engraved with the words "No one loved gorillas more."

The mystery of who killed Dian Fossey still is unsolved today. In August 1986, an ex-employee of Karisoke named Emmanuel Rwelekana, and Wayne McGuire, an American researcher, were charged with the murder. By this time McGuire had fled to the United States, and within weeks Rwelekana was found hanged in his cell. Many people believe both men were scapegoats, and suggest that poachers killed Fossey. Names in high places were probably passed to Fossey by the poacher Sebahutu, and some believe she was silenced before she could reveal them. There is also the theory that Fossey had to be stopped before she threatened gorilla tourism. Unfortunately, the truth will probably never be known.

ABOVE: *Fossey always said she would like to be buried in the gorilla graveyard. Today the plot is almost overgrown with trees and shrubs.*

ABOVE: *A tourist quietly watches the antics of two young gorillas. It isn't always possible to visit the gorillas now, but we can help to conserve them by supporting the Dian Fossey Gorilla Fund.*

Fossey's love for the gorillas is a lasting legacy. The Digit Fund is now known as the Dian Fossey Gorilla Fund. Through sponsorship of the gorillas and fund-raising activities, it supports scientific research projects and field studies. This data advances our knowledge of the gorillas and helps conservationists understand how best to do their work.

Anti-poaching activities are still vital, but now local people are actively involved in protecting the gorilla. Through small-scale businesses based around the gorilla habitat, they have found a means of making a living—their survival is based upon the gorillas' survival.

The task is made difficult by the civil war that has been raging on and off in Rwanda since 1994. Since this time, workers at Karisoke have had to leave on countless occasions. With an estimated 650 mountain gorillas left in central Africa, war has now become as serious a threat to the gorillas' survival as poaching, destruction of their natural habitat, and human activities.

IN THEIR OWN WORDS

"If we do not act now to protect them, most populations of great ape will become extinct within the next twenty years."

A VIEW PUT FORWARD BY THE SPEAKERS AT THE LAUNCH OF *2001—AN APE ODYSSEY* FROM *DIGIT NEWS*, THE MAGAZINE FOR THE DIAN FOSSEY GORILLA FUND, WINTER 2000.

The Legacy of Dian Fossey

"This goes beyond the bounds of strict science.... Just after Fossey's death, three gorilla groups who had been at some distance from Visoke suddenly homed in on the mountain. One group traveled almost continually for two days to arrive in the vicinity."

SCIENTIST IAN REDMOND TOLD THIS STORY AT THE *NATIONAL GEOGRAPHIC* MEMORIAL BENEFIT TO FOSSEY. HE'D BEEN ASKED HOW THE GORILLAS HAD REACTED TO FOSSEY'S DEATH (FROM *WALKING WITH THE GREAT APES* BY SY MONTGOMERY).

DIAN FOSSEY WAS the first scientist to conduct a long-term close-up study of the mountain gorillas in their natural habitat in central Africa. Her pioneering work in the field means we now know something of their family structure, their behavior, including body language and vocalizations, their diet, and their favored habitat. In her book *Gorillas in the Mist,* she introduced us to these gentle creatures that share 98 percent of our genes and so many of our own characteristics.

The Human Ape

While Fossey was working in the field, other scientists were publishing work about human behavior. In 1967, British scientist Desmond Morris wrote a best-selling book, *The Human Ape.* This enjoyable book traced human behavior back to our animal ancestors. Ultimately our fascination with ourselves has become another reason to understand and

RIGHT: *The mountain gorilla is an endangered species. The future of young gorillas such as this one depends on ongoing conservation efforts.*

PRIMATE EYES

By making comparisons with other primates, humans continue to gain an insight into our evolution. In 2001, scientists in Japan were trying to understand why humans have white around the iris of the eye, while in other primates the same area is dark. In the past, scientists believed that apes had dark eyes to protect them from the sun. They've since discovered that nocturnal primates also have dark eyes and have concluded that the darkness of the eye is to disguise the animal's direction of gaze—in other words it's a defense mechanism. With humans, the eyes have great social significance. Looking into the eyes of the person you're talking to gives further information about what he or she is thinking.

protect our fellow primates. Each year we try to understand more about our evolution by discovering more about apes. Scientists have tried to find out if apes could speak. They have discovered that these highly intelligent creatures do not have the right organs to talk, but that they can learn sign language. We are still trying to discover who our closest relatives are—the gorilla or the chimpanzee. With only 650 mountain gorillas left in the world, we are running out of time. But the most important thing is saving the gorillas from extinction for their own sake.

Timeline

470 B.C.

What was probably the first written reference to gorillas is found in the autographical book *The Voyage of Hanno the Carthaginian.*

1625

Andrew Battell, an English explorer, writes about an encounter with a strange animal, possibly a gorilla, in West Africa.

1758

Carl Linnaeus recognizes the close relationship between humans, monkeys, and apes. He classified these species as primates.

1847

American missionary Thomas Savage and anatomist Jeffries Wyman discover a new species of ape, called a gorilla.

Circa 1857

American traveler Paul Belloni du Chaillu attempts what is probably the first ever gorilla hunt using guns. He wrote, "He reminded me of nothing but some hellish dream creature—a being of that hideous order, half man, half beast."

1859

Charles Darwin publishes *On the Origin of Species by Means of Natural Selection or the Preservation of Favored Races in the Struggle for Life.*

1871

Charles Darwin publishes *The Descent of Man.*

1902

A German army officer named Captain Oscar von Beringe shoots two unknown species of ape while climbing Mount Sabinyo in the Virungas Volcanoes. One body was recovered and it became the type specimen—the specimen against which other specimens would be compared in future scientific research—for *Gorilla gorilla beringei*, or mountain gorilla.

1931

Louis Leakey begins archaeological digs at Olduvai Gorge in Tanzania. Ancient tools are discovered.

1932

JANUARY 16: Dian Fossey is born in Fairfax, California.

1938

Fossey's parents, George and Kitty, get divorced.

1950

Fossey becomes a pre-veterinary medical student at the University of California.

1954

Fossey graduates from San Jose State College with a degree in occupational therapy.

1959

Louis Leakey's wife, Mary Leakey, discovers bones of a species of early man called *Zinjanthropus*.

1959–1960

George Schaller first observes mountain gorillas at Kabara.

1960

Louis Leakey discovers the skull, hands, and feet of a species called *Homo habilis*. Jane Goodall arrives at Gombe in Tanzania to begin field studies of chimpanzees.

1963

SEPTEMBER: Fossey first visits Africa, where she meets Dr. Louis Leakey and visits the gorillas at Kabara in the Congo.

1966

MARCH: Fossey meets Dr. Leakey at a lecture in Louisville, Kentucky.
DECEMBER: Fossey returns to Kabara, within Virungas Park in the Democratic Republic of the Congo in Africa, to begin studying the mountain gorilla.

1967

JULY: Fossey is forced to leave Kabara.
SEPTEMBER: Fossey founds the Karisoke Research Center.

1968

JANUARY: Fossey writes to Louis Leakey to tell him she has completed 485 hours of observation of the mountain gorilla.

JUNE/JULY: Alan Root from *National Geographic* films Fossey and the gorillas. He is replaced by Bob Campbell in August.

AUGUST: Fossey's father, George, commits suicide.

1969

FEBRUARY: Fossey saves the lives of Coco and Pucker, the two orphaned gorillas stolen by poachers for a German zoo.

1970

JANUARY: Fossey first makes human contact with a mountain gorilla named Peanuts.

Fossey starts studying for a Ph.D. at Cambridge University in England.

1972

Louis Leakey dies.

1977

DECEMBER: Digit is murdered. Fossey subsequently starts the Digit Fund to raise money for anti-poaching activities.

1978

JANUARY: David Attenborough and the BBC film crew encounter the mountain gorilla.

JULY: The bodies of Uncle Bert and Macho from Group 4 are found, killed by poachers.

1979

FEBRUARY: Fossey receives a telegram from the *National Geographic*. It expresses concern at her anti-poaching activities. A few days later, the U.S. Secretary of State cabled the ambassador to Rwanda to request that Fossey leave Rwanda.

1980

Fossey begins teaching at Cornell University in Ithaca, New York.

1981

APRIL: Dian Fossey, Jane Goodall, and Birute Galdikas (Louis Leakey's "trimates") present a lecture at Sweet Briar College in Virginia: "What We Can Learn about Humankind from the Apes."

1983

JUNE: Fossey returns to Karisoke for the first time in three years.

AUGUST: *Gorillas in the Mist* is published.

1984

OCTOBER: Fossey is presented with the Joseph Wood Krutch Medal in recognition of her work with the gorillas at the Human Society's convention in San Diego.

1985

Fossey appears on "The Tonight Show" with Johnny Carson.

DECEMBER 27: Fossey is murdered.

DECEMBER 31: Fossey is buried in the gorilla graveyard in Karisoke.

1986

American Ruth Morris Keesling sets up Morris Animal Foundation's Mountain Gorilla Veterinary Center in Rwanda.

1988

The film *Gorillas in the Mist* tells the story of Fossey's life. It is an international success.

1990

Karisoke is evacuated as civil war in Rwanda begins.

1994

Karisoke is evacuated once more as the civil war in Rwanda escalates.

1996

The Dian Fossey Gorilla Fund launches a new project at Mount Tshiaberimu in the Congo and a community conservation program in Rwanda.

Glossary

Appendicitis An infection of the appendix that is very painful and requires surgery to remove the appendix.

Assassination The planned murder of a person—usually somebody famous.

Black magic Magic used for evil purposes.

Bush, the Land that is covered in native trees and shrubs or other vegetation, and usually has a low human population.

Civil war War between rival groups within one nation, usually because of religious or political differences.

Conservator Somebody who protects nature and wildlife.

Data collection The collection of information, such as measurements and different behavior, for scientific purposes.

Defense mechanism Behavior, such as barking when frightened, or characteristics, like giving off unpleasant smells when attacked, that help animals protect themselves during confrontations with other animals.

Doctorate The highest university degree in any subject.

DNA The chemicals inside plant and animal cells in which the genes are found.

Dysentery A disease of the intestines that causes diarrhea with blood.

Evolution The process by which a species (both animals and plants) develops from earlier forms.

Extinction When an entire species of animal or plant has died out completely.

Foliage Leaves, flowers, and branches.

Game Animals hunted for meat.

Genes The things inside animal and plant cells that determine what they will be like, for example, in humans there are genes for eye, skin, and hair color.

Gorilla safaris Specially organized trips for tourists to see the mountain gorillas in their natural habitat.

High altitude Usually refers to land that is above 12,000 feet. Being at high altitude can cause sickness, headaches, and shortness of breath.

Homo habilis The scientific term used to describe an early representation of human beings.

Homo sapiens The scientific term used to describe the most modern representation of human beings.

Itinerary A plan for travel, including routes and times.

Knuckleprints The impression left by the knuckles of an animal on a surface, for example in the soil.

Massacre The savage killing of large numbers of people or animals.

Matriarch A female of a species who is the head of the group.

Natural habitat The place where animals can live freely with access to their normal diet and surroundings.

Nocturnal Animals that are active at night.

Occupational therapy Therapy by means of creative activity, prescribed for recovery and rehabilitation.

Paleoanthropologist Someone who studies the origins, physical characteristics, behavior, and social relationships of primates from fossil evidence.

Pneumonia A serious lung disease.

Poacher Somebody who illegally hunts animals or fish.

Political unrest When the politics of a country make its citizens likely to revolt.

Pre-veterinary medicine Studies that lead to an entry into a veterinarian curriculum.

Primates A group of mammals that includes lemurs, tarsiers, monkeys, apes, and humans.

Savannah Grassland area with a few trees and shrubs.

Scapegoat A person who is made to take the blame for somebody else's wrongdoings.

Sponsors A group or company that provides money to support a cause or charity.

Statistics Information and facts expressed as numbers or percentages.

Submissive Obedient and willing to give in to others.

Subspecies A term used to classify animals. Gorilla, for example, is the name of the species. The subspecies of gorilla are western lowland, eastern lowland, and mountain.

Swahili A language of East Africa that is the official language of Kenya and Tanzania but used widely in central Africa, too.

Thesis An extended essay based on research that is submitted as part of a degree or diploma.

Tracker A person who is especially trained to search for wild animals by following scents or marks such as footprints.

Vegetation A collective word for plants.

Vocalizations Expressions of different moods by using voices or noises.

Zoology The study of animals.

Further Information

BOOKS FOR YOUNGER READERS

Freedman, Suzanne. *Innovative Minds: Dian Fossey: Befriending the Gorillas.* New York: Raintree Steck-Vaughn Publishers, 1997.

Schaller, George B. *Light Shining Through the Mist: A Photobiography of Dian Fossey.* Washington, D.C.: National Geographic Society, 1998.

Schott, Jane A. *Dian Fossey.* Minneapolis, MN: Carolrhoda Books Inc., 2001.

Wood, Richard. *Groundbreakers: Scientists and Inventors: Dian Fossey.* Chicago, IL: Heinemann Library, 2001.

BOOKS FOR OLDER READERS

Fossey, Dian. *Gorillas in the Mist.* Boston, MA: Mariner Books, 2000.

Montgomery, Sy. *Walking with the Great Apes: Jane Goodall, Dian Fossey, Birute Galdikas.* Boston, MA: Mariner Books, 1992.

Mowat, Farley. *Woman in the Mists: The Story of Dian Fossey and the Mountain Gorillas of Africa.* New York: Warner Books, 1988.

Naden, Corinne J. *Gateway Green Biography: Dian Fossey: At Home with the Giant Gorillas.* Brookfield, CT: Millbrook Press Inc., 2002.

WEBSITES

www.gorillafund.org
You can adopt a gorilla or give to this charity for the mountain gorillas. A newsletter called Digit News is published a few times a year. It and the site give updates on the current situation for the gorillas in Rwanda, including exciting snippets such as the birth of new gorillas.

www.unmuseum.org/fossey.htm
This site tells the story of Dian Fossey and discusses highlights of her study of the gorillas in the Virungas volcanoes in Rwanda.

www.primates-online.com
Includes a special section just for kids, including a PCWS Kids' Club where you can sign up for a free subscription to the newsletter *Faces from the Forest.*

http://animal.discovery.com/cams/gorillavid.html
Live video of gorillas at Franklin Park Zoo in Boston. You may need to download special software to enjoy this fun site.

Index

Page numbers in **bold** are pages where there is a photograph or an illustration.